THE RUINED MAN
CHAPTER ONE

By Christopher Whitney

Copyright © 2017 by Christopher Whitney

All rights reserved. No part of this publication may be reproduced, distributed, or transmitted in any form or by any means, including photocopying, recording, or other electronic or mechanical methods, without the prior written permission of the publisher, except in the case of brief quotations embodied in critical reviews and certain other non-commercial uses permitted by copyright law.

First Edition

Book 1 in The Ruined Man Series by Christopher Whitney

Visit the author's Official Facebook page:
www.facebook.com/TheRuinedManOriginal

This is a work of fiction. Names, characters, places, and incidents either are the products of the author's imagination or are used fictitiously. Any resemblance to actual persons, living or dead, businesses, companies, events, or locales is entirely coincidental.

DEDICATION

I Dedicate this book to my Facebook Followers. Thank You all for inspiring me to pick my soul up off the ground and find the strength to believe in a future again. I could not have done it without your support. It has been a hard and testing journey for me and there were times when I felt like I was completely alone. You have all helped me to see that there are many of us on this path through pain, and I will forever be happy that you were and are a part of my life.

Thank You, so very much.

Love Christopher

Think of this as a Preface, if you will.

My name is Christopher, and this is my book. The first of many, I hope! This book is meant to be read in small doses, something to warm a cold day or pass time when it seems to have stopped ticking. This book is for all who need to see that you do not walk alone with your feelings or any of those confusing emotions that may swirl around inside of you like a wild storm.

I want to take a moment, to explain to you what you will find inside this book *(Or Journal, depending on how you look at it.)* as to me, this is more than just a collection of poetry and muddled words.

It is a Journey.

My Journey, and perhaps yours too.

Inside you will find many of my pieces that I originally published up onto my Facebook page (TheRuinedManOriginal) and though some of them remain the same, others are altered, rewritten, extended, edited, or just completely different. There are some new pieces too.

It is my hope that you will come with me on the journey through this book and that perhaps it may help you to heal as I have tried to heal, or at the very least it will offer new perspectives to situations and feelings that often seem too confusing to put words behind.

Thank You for being here,

Thank you for believing in me.

Sincerely,

Christopher Whitney,

AKA, The Ruined Man.

TABLE OF CONTENT

PART ONE: FAVOURITES

PART TWO: BACK STORIES

PART THREE: RAWNESS

PART FOUR: THERAPY OF INK

PART FIVE: SHOCK

PART SIX: A COLD REALITY

PART SEVEN: PAIN

PART EIGHT: HURT

PART NINE: LOVE

PART TEN: PASSION

PART ELEVEN: SCRAPS OF ME

PART TWELVE: QUESTIONS

PART THIRTEEN: EXCLUSIVES

PART FOURTEEN: FINAL WORDS

PART ONE

F A V O U R I T E S

"My Heart feels so heavy, it is sinking into the pit of my stomach, and crushing all the butterflies beneath it's broken weight."

Author's Note: This first collection of pieces are my personal favourites. Pieces that I often go back and read to myself. Writing them provoked a lot of passion, emotion, and reactions out of Me, they were written during especially dark periods of time in my life and each piece has it's own special place in my heart. I share these pieces to start my book because I know that this journey is going to take us through many dark forests of words and I wanted to start with a few things that I find to be beautiful before we get into the deep ugly rawness. Please enjoy them, and keep an eye out for my Author's Notes to learn little titbits of information behind the words.

I Won't Move

I will stand on the sidelines, watch you forgetting me.

I will watch you drift away, get on with your life,

and fade from sight.

But I Won't Move.

I will stand here until the day I die,

Forever hoping that one day,

You will Remember Me

Author's Note: This next piece was written a year after I wrote "I Won't Move" and it still amazes me how the contrast between the emotions changed so much from there to here.

I Did Not Move

The sky is bleeding a thousand colours, and my eyes are crying, a thousand more.

I catch the rain, in my hands, and they break the silence, of our ending.

You have taken everything, and there is nothing left of me.

It must have made you feel so good, to watch me bleed for you.

Now you run, far from me, and I just stand here still.

You have shown me the difference between love and hate,

And I see that there is little difference at all.

Christopher Whitney

Black & Purple

Darkness surrounds Me,

The poisonous embrace of demonic infestations.

Shadows gasp as I pass through them,

in violating declension.

Monsters and ghosts corrupt the light,

Blooming black roses and Purple stars.

By Christopher Whitney

Author's Note: One sunny day, somebody asked me, what it felt like when love died. I could not answer them, I stared at them in silence for a couple of moments and then I just behaved like they had never asked the question at all, changing the subject and asking them about the weather. Later that night, I sat home on my own, drinking whiskey, brooding, and stuffs … and that question was still haunting me, I ended up grabbing one of my journals, and drunkenly scribbling this next piece down.

How does it feel to me when love dies?

It feels like drinking an apocalypse from a broken bottle that cuts my lips and turns me into a wasteland of dead feathers.

It feels like swallowing silence and hearing it scream its way down my throat.

It feels like everything, and nothing, the shadows, and the light.

And now that the love is dead,

I walk a road of fractured memories,

Tears of crimson acid falling from my eyes,

dissolving the ground from beneath my feet.

I fall into any abyss beneath the bottomless pits of hell.

The Corrosive Fire.

You play with dangerous things, little girl. Some dangers don't have a fire that burns bright like all the others,

Some times it is a corrosive simmer that will boil you down to steam,

before you even know you've touched the heat.

By Christopher Whitney

Deep in the Magic

By Christopher Whitney

Lightning flickers and snaps in my eyes,

Around pupils of a shuddering black moon.

I feel thunder trembling through my limbs,

Fingers tightening around the throat of this life.

A growl settles in my throat and a feral glare is cast upon the path ahead.

I take one step, and the wind blows,

I take another, and it holds it's breath.

My Goal Appears,

Deep in the magic of dreams.

I see it now, and so does my spirit.

I am coming, says my soul.

I am coming, For You.

Defiance

By Christopher Whitney

I am on the fence about fate.

Some times I believe in it,

But there are times when I do not want to.

I sit and wonder why I am like this,

And why I have these contradicting thoughts,

I realise that as with many things,

It always leads back to You.

You see, I do believe in fate,

But only if you are Mine.

If it is fate that we are meant to be,

Then I am full of faith and a true believer.

But if it is fated that we will never be,

Then I stand in defiance of fate,

And I will write our Own.

CURSED

I am cursed.

With a heart that knows no bounds.

I am cursed to give all of me, every grain..

To those who cannot even handle a drop of Me.

I am cursed to love more,

than any of the love I will ever receive.

I am cursed to forever love You,

Even though you will never love me.

Christopher Whitney

Author's Note: As you may have guessed by the title, I wrote this next one during a time when I was intoxicated with a bottle of whiskey. I was in a playful mood, but a melancholy one too.

The Drunken Poet

By Christopher Whitney

It is the night that is the worst, the hardest part of all,

I think that it's nocturnal, when lonely starts to call.

Once the sun begins to set, with sadness in every bone,

I look around this empty house, and know that I'm alone.

Now I don't mind the loneliness, it's nothing new to Me,

I'll pour myself a whiskey, because I can't quite drink the tea.

I turn off all the lights, and then I start to drink,

I close my eyes to hide the truth, but you are all I think.

It is then I start to miss you, as I pour another shot,

Drinking hard to remind me, that you love me not.

The Most Beautiful

I love her so very much,

But these days I just keep it to myself.

And loving in absolute silence,

is the most beautiful pain,

that ever killed me.

I am fire, and she is gasoline.

But I choose to burn,

and as the ashes begin to fall,

I close my eyes, and fall for her.

Christopher Whitney

Dim......

For the longest time I felt like I was crazy for feeling things as strongly as I do.

Now I am starting to see that you were the crazy one, for not feeling anything at all.

You should never give up on what makes you feel your soul.

Some can live their entire life, perfectly content,

and yet never feel their soul burning inside of them.

To some a soul is still a myth,

So if you can feel yours glowing,

Don't let it dim.

…... Christopher Whitney

F I R E

By Christopher Whitney

It wasn't Love. It never was.

I don't know, why I didn't know,

Much sooner than this,

But we are just not meant to be.

I am a fire,

wild and free.

But you are an ocean,

cold and stormy.

I engulfed you in warmth,

and you drowned me in the shallows.

But I am still a fire,

And I don't want your ocean,

To drown out my flames.

So I am letting you go,

Before the Fire of Me,

Turns to ash.

Author's Note: I wrote this next piece one night after reading 'FIRE' and to me, it feels like an encore to the feelings that I once expressed when I wrote 'FIRE' It is the same subject, the same fire, but different flames, and I like that change in perspective. I decided to share it because I hope that you can appreciate that too.

FIRE: ENCORE

"The fire crackles inside of me, licking at the rafters of my hollowed out ribcage. I walk in a world that is foreign to me. I am desolate in it's rapture, damned in its miracle. I don't belong here, this place of vultures and thieves. If I am to fall to this, If I am to lose, it will not be gentle, and there will be no mercy. I will kick and scream until I am spent, and when there is nothing left inside of me. I will use these ashes to blacken my skin and become the shadow of my own fate."

Better Than Me

By Christopher Whitney

Today I feel a mess, Chaos of anarchy and all that hides between. My mind is haunted with insignificance, my tongue is silenced by the loss of fire.

I am so very tired of feeling exhausted.

If only I could fix myself, with tape and gum, just enough to hold it together for a fraction of the peace I want back.

But I do not recognize myself, and my soul has fled for the hills. Perhaps it will find a better place, where it will be noticed, understood, and worth something.

Perhaps it will find a place,

That is Better Than Me.

I Would Love

By Christopher Whitney

I would love to be the sun, as it pours all over You.

And the moisture on your lips, I would love to be that too.

I would love to be the wind, That blows on through your hair.

I would love it if you knew, That I will always be there.

I would love to be your summer, And winter, and spring, and fall.

I would love to be your someone, And I would love to be your all.

You ask me what love is and I cannot tell you.

Because love for me, might be different for you. But I do know that it is more than just sweaty sex and physical intimacy. We all have a basic idea about what love is, but there are more layers to it than most people understand.

Love isn't always about happiness,

or only about the good feelings.

Love is also pain, the way in which you let another hurt you because you love them enough to forgive them and give them another chance even though most think you are foolish to do so.

Love is some times the absence of somebody and yet still, you choose to wait for them, for as long as it takes. Love is about the ups, and the downs, the fights you are willing to fight, and the defeats you are willing to accept. Love is the moon and how it glows brightly even in it's darkest hour. Love is the lost puppy, that finds its way home against all odds. Love is that smile on your face when you wake up in the morning and see that sleeping face next to you. Love is a great many things and love is nothing at all. Love is an act, and love is a feeling, some times when you can't feel anything else, and some times when you feel too much.

Love is constant and it never dies.

Love is what you make it, and how you see it.

Love can be what you want it to be.

It is up to You.

But you ask me what Love is to Me, and the simplest way I know of answering that is to tell you that when you asked me that question, She was all that came to mind.

No Harder Defeat

By Christopher Whitney

I am trapped within a battlefield of my own soul. My demons fight my pieces and they cut me down at every turn. The darkness of the sun shrouds me like a blanket of hate. I tried to run, I tried to do all that I could to avoid the inevitability of losing myself amidst all the fighting.

I can stand right in front of you and you will hear nothing. But I hear it, I hear it all, the clashing of swords, slashing of talons, the screams of the fallen, and all that I hold within me. It doesn't matter what I do, or where I turn, I just cannot seem to win this war. I have used strategy, willpower, and at times nothing more than survival. But my army is wearing thin as the pieces of me fall away, Slew by the demons that you created in my heart when you broke it in two and let all that pain out.

It was a portal to another world, a nightmare world, one where nothing grows and there is no air to breathe.

It is a dismal world of hurt and I have been swallowed by it now.

But what else can I do if not reach for my weapon and try to find my feet for one last wave of onslaught. The only thing I know, is fighting. Because I have been fighting all of my life, to find You, to keep you, and now I must lose you,

no matter how much I fight,

no matter how many deaths I live through,

I must lose You.

And I know no harder defeat than that.

KOMOREBI

By Christopher Whitney

The sunlight filters through the trees, and reaches out
to touch my face. I close my eyes and kiss the tears,
as the golden warmth falls short of my heart.

The day brings with it a great many things. The birds
wake to hunt the worms, as their offspring sing and
chirp in their nests. The scent of early hours flares my
nostrils, a mixture of bark, rain, and the sun. The leafs
of green all around still glisten with the morning dew.
The sky is caught in transition from black to blue and
the world is starting to wake up.

But the day doesn't bring You. Not to me. And so I
turn from the day, to find a cave, or a dark place,
within which I can hide, Until the night comes, in
hopes that when the moon returns,

you will return with it.

To my arms, my life, and my heart.

"You were a golden glass of dreams and I drank you like a shot of spiced whiskey on a cold winter's night. The snow was falling but we were on fire."

Christopher Whitney

PART TWO

BACK STORIES

*"The hour grows late, and all the lonely hearts are
out there, thinking about somebody else."*

Author's Note: This next collection, is going to be focused on the pieces I have written that carry a bit of back story to them. Pieces that are extremely relevant to me -because- of that back story. For each piece, I will add a little note titled: Back Story, to tell you a little bit about it. Enjoy!

I can feel my soul inside of me, it is a sun, a burning wolf with fire in it's howl.

I can feel your soul inside of You,

Glowing brightly, with the phantom flames of the moon.

And my wolf searches for Yours,

To start their own pack,

Just You and Me,

Them & Us.

Living Wild and Free in the Forest of our dreams.

BACK STORY: I wrote this one in pitch darkness. It was late at night and the curtains were closed. The lights switched off. And the bedroom was just black. I had a strange dream that woke me up and I scrambled to feel around for pen and paper, scribbling this down. In the dream, I was a wolf and I was running as fast as the wind through a forest, faster than a cheetah, faster than anything alive. It was dark in the forest, but I could see, I am not sure if that was because I had wolf eyes, or something else, but there was a blue glow around me that allowed me to weave through the trees and leap over the wild berry bushes. I was chasing something, a beautiful golden being that was moving just a tiny bit faster than me. But the being wasn't as smooth as me and couldn't move through the trees quite as flawlessly, it kept hesitating to scramble through the bushes, catching itself on the thorns, this allowed me to catch up. And mere moments before I could spring onto it, it zipped up towards the sky at rocket speed. I watched it flying towards the stars like a meteor. That golden shimmer transforming into blue flames until eventually it exploded on the dark horizon up above, and sitting there in it's place, was the moon. And I howled... I will never forget that dream.

For Less

You never had the courage for Me,

You were too cowardly to pursue somebody who was worth pursuing.

Instead, you pursued somebody who was convenient.

You dared not to take a risk for Me,

Instead, you shared your bed with the safer option.

You were too impatient to wait for Me,

Instead, You chose easy, as opposed to happiness.

You wouldn't settle for Me,

Instead, You settled for Less.

BACK STORY: Ohhh, this one. Even now, as I read back through it I am just struck with the PTSD of memories that tore my soul into pieces. This poem, I wrote on the day I discovered.... well... you figure it out... In any case, it deserved to be here.

Don't go for the one who promises you a world of fantasies that they can never deliver.

Go for the one who makes reality better than any far sailing fantasy you could possibly imagine.

People have a trick, of playing nice until they come to learn what it is that you dream of, and then they reshape themselves to be that, and pretend to be what you need.

Do not fall for the fakes, or the salesman trying to sell you dreams.

Go with what is Real,

And then You will see,

That fantasies pale, when faced with real and raw mutual love.

BACK STORY: I wrote this untitled piece after somebody asked me to write a poem for them. It is not really how it works for me, I cannot just write for the sake of writing, because to me, that isn't poetry. Poetry has to be felt, it has to bleed onto the paper by itself. So instead of a poem, I wrote them some advice. I didn't find it to be anything special, but when I gave it to them, they broke down into tears and thanked me, and that was a profound time for me, because I realised that people don't always need to be given exactly what they ask for, some times, they just need to be shown, that they are not invisible, that somebody sees them, even when they cannot see themselves.

The Ice Heart

My demons used to weigh me down,

chew me up and spit me out,

with their voices loud,

and claws like razors,

They always won,

I always lost.

And their wicked smiles,

spoke of my defeat.

Now I walk with my chin held high,

and my demons run,

when they see me coming.

For I would rather set my soul on fire,

and watch it burn to ashes,

before I ever fall to my demons again.

I bury myself behind a wall of titanium,

to make sure anyone who looks my way,

sees only a stoical beast.

I won't show weakness, and I won't back down,

Because through life I walk,

With a Heart of ice, and a soul of Fire.

BACK STORY: This poem was based upon a fictional character that I came up with. I was in the mood for writing a story, rather than poetry. But I could not come up with a character that I wished to write about. I had writers block, and for those who feel the need to express through writing, you know that writing block really sucks. Well I spent many days trying to come up with a character but just could not settle on it, and eventually, I gave up and decided to write some more poetry instead. And the very first poetry piece I wrote after that decision, was this one, and it gave birth to a character that I write some of my most favourite stories about. Stories that are just for me. So that's why it is here, because it gave me the character I could never find. When I needed it the most. I will never forget that character, or this poem, and I will never forget how he didn't come when I tried to force it, but instead came when the time was right. And those are the best types of characters to come up with, not the ones you create and force, but the ones that come as if they have been there all along.

PART THREE

RAWNESS

"My heart is bleeding bitter rain drops of cold tender misery"

Author's Note: In this section you will find pieces that I wrote whilst feeling very raw. There were no revisions, no pause for composure. I felt raw, I grabbed a pen, and I began to write. No holding back, no filters, and no censoring.

To Never Go

What do You Do,

When a home is not a house,

Not a place at all?

What do you do,

When home is a person?

What do you do,

When that person evicts you?

And you do not know,

How to never go home again.

And when hope died,

Everything else followed behind it,

Like a mass suicide

Of all the things you ever gave to me,

Dreams, Desires, Ambitions, and Goals.

I never knew that would be the price,

But from the Moment I loved you,

I never did think,

To think twice.

Christopher Whitney

I.

I sit alone in this dark and quiet room, and I know now better than I ever did before, that I am not getting over this, I'm just getting used to it. I am becoming numb to the earth shattering agony of your absence. It hurts like hellfire, and it is becoming the only thing that I can even feel. I am stabbed in the spine by the stark realisation that the people in my life, who have hurt me the most, are the same people who I have loved the most.

Now they are all gone, and I see that I have been a complete and utter fool for you. I sacrificed all of my world, to see your face, and then you abandoned me, only when I had nothing left. The exhaustion is overwhelming. I keep trying to feed my heart whiskey, To rob it blind of all your memories, but it doesn't work. I can't even breathe properly without You. I opened up my door for you, and lowered down my walls. I believed you would be different, that you could be trusted. But you walked in, wrecked everything, and then walked back out the door,

leaving my love and trust in festering ruins behind You.

I AM A VIKING

My heart is guarded by a shield wall.

My truth is an axe and it will cleave your lies in two.

My honour will pillage the ruins of your betrayal and my love will burn it to the ground.

By Christopher Whitney

"I know that you think I am weak, and to you I might never mean much of anything, But you are wrong, we were not a mistake. You can say what you want about Me, cut me down all that you want. But don't you stand there, looking at me like that and telling me that we were wrong. What we had was the -only- thing in my entire life that was ever right. It was Real. For Me. And if you ever loved me back, I don't know how you can say any of these horrible things to me. You mean everything to me, and your words cut like knives, and you act like we weren't real, but only love can hurt like this. We have been through so much together and we always come through, because I choose you, and you choose me. That's how we always survive this. Because we never stop fighting for each other. And this... This doesn't have to be the end of us. Because I am right here, standing right in front of You. I love You and I will love you for all of my life, I want this, and I want you. So whatever it takes, let's just go back to choosing each other and we can get through-"

"Stop." … She said, cutting me off. She looked me in the eyes and finished with … "I just don't love you any more."

Authors Note: *The piece you just read is part of an unpublished novel that I once wrote, I wanted to share this piece with you, because it is very powerful* *to me. The unpublished novel is called "The Price of Souls" and I share quotes from it every once in a while on my Facebook page. I have been asked why I do not release it or if I ever will and I never have an answer. It's a complicated situation for me, for one thing, the story is written in first person view and though it all makes sense to me, it likely wouldn't to anybody else because in my head I know about all the other things that happened off screen so to speak. Things that wouldn't fit in a first person view kind of book because the main character was not present. And without those things, the story appears incomplete. So in order for me to release it, I would have to rewrite it from scratch, in third person view and put in those other important scenes that make the pieces fit together fully. And that's one big reason why I have not released it. Another reason is that it is very long, it is over one hundred and fifty chapters long (LOL! True story!) so I would need to split it into multiple books. The most important reason of my decision to so far not release it is because there is a lot of ME in that story. It is a work of fiction but there are some parts in it taken from my own life, my own memories, and that makes it a very personal, raw, and vulnerable story to expose. One day, I might release it, but knowing what a huge undertaking it would be to get it ready, I am just focusing on Poetry right now and would like to complete The Ruined Man series first.*

How sad to know,

that I'm becoming part of your past.

How invigorating to know,

that you will never see my future.

NO RULES

By Christopher Whitney

There are no rules when it comes to love,

There is only the fight,

And how far you are willing to go,

Or how far you are not.

Understand, what that really means is,

How much Love is worth to you,

And how much it is not.

And the thing with loving you,

Is that I have been left a little emptier,

Than I ever was before.

And a little too broken,

To ever feel whole again.

Just Not Right Now.

By Christopher Whitney

You are gone, but you used to be Mine.

I still sing songs about you in the chambers of my heart.

A place where nobody can reach, a place that will always belong to You.

And I still speak to the Gods about You.

You know I'm not religious, I never really was.

But I speak to them, All of Them.

I speak of my love and ask them to take all of Mine,

And wrap up your heart with it so that you will be safe and sound.

Every night I look to the moon, I see the stars,

And I wonder if they are watching over you too,

Bathing you in their glow.

For now I stay here, in the shadows around your soul,

    Fighting back the darkness and telling it,

        it can not have You.

        Because you are Mine,

        Just not right now.

The Shores of Never Lasting

By Christopher Whitney

You are like a golden beach, a sea shore,

and every time I come to you, I am pulled away.

Like a tide.

But I keep coming back,

I keep laying kisses at your feet,

Only to be sent away again.

I am never allowed to stay.

And I never stop coming back.

This is what it is like,

to be the ocean,

and unable to drown,

in my own dark waters.

Authors Note: This next piece was my very first attempt at Haiku poetry. It is a form of poetry where each segment must be three lines long, and follow this pattern: First line, five syllables. Second line, seven syllables. Third Line, five syllables.

Let's

Let's lay together,

I don't care where, Don't care why,

As long as it's You.

Let's Talk about us,

Let's talk nothings, and some things,

I want you, with Me.

Let's fall asleep now,

And wake up with new mornings,

Two souls, and one life.

NIGHTMARE COCKTAIL

By Christopher Whitney

You are a nightmare cocktail,

All of my favourite things poured into one life.

But you batter my heart with my greatest fears.

You are every dream I ever wanted.

But you fill my head with nightmares.

You rub your soul up against Mine.

But you stay out of my reach.

You pepper my feelings with your knives,

But you turn away when I start to bleed.

NOT WORTH

THE EYES ARE NOT WORTH THE TEARS,

THE HEART IS NOT WORTH THE PAIN,

AND YOU, ARE NOT WORTH THE ME.

The Numbing Jar.

By Christopher Whitney

I pace up and down the empty hallway of this empty house.

Another shard of glass falls from my mind and shatters across the splintered floor.

Emotions storm through me like translucent surges of thunder.

I go from angry, to hurt, and then all the way back to sorrow.

I fade in and out of reality like a flickering bulb.

I am a mess of chaotic lightning. Snapping and Cracking.

Lighting up the darkness for a fraction, only to be swallowed by the shadows

in the very next breath.

The Long Howl

By Christopher Whitney

You chose him, and that is fine. But we both know that even if he loved you for a hundred and one lives, he still wouldn't love you as much as I do on any given night.

So settle for your less, if you please. That makes no difference to me. I will still howl your name to the moon and hope the wolf in you one day returns my call.

From Out of Reach

By Christopher Whitney

It was not my choice to love, but it was your damned choice to leave.

Now I sit here in the rain, watching the moon as I always do when I miss you.

I see it far away, up in that all black,

Casting that haunting presence down across this world and yet never able to quite reach out and touch any of it.

I see now, that this is how I was always meant to love You...

From afar,

From Loneliness,

From out of reach.

PART FOUR

THERAPY OF INK

"*My soul is like an ocean wave, crashing against the rocky cliffs of my heart*"

Author's Note: It is no secret that I very much believe writing is one of the best forms of therapy. And this section will contain pieces that I wrote to myself in order to try and process my storm of emotions enough to get through. I have faced some hard days where I did not even want to get out of bed, let alone do anything else. So some times I write to myself, to encourage myself, or at the very least just to try and clear my head enough to think straight.

The Rambles of Insanity

I seek no words, merely a glimpse, beyond the depths of paramour. I disturb the silence more than the memories, as I boldly step into the unknown. I walk a forest of burning trees. Forever searching for not peace, but pieces, of your soul and mine, in the place they met their ends.

In the whispering whispers of the frozen lake, there stirs a slither of delightfully detrimental hope. Upon the banks of the cracked and frosty shores, there lies the gentle & gallant scent of Petrichor.

And within all of this, I have come to realize that we often feel as though we have high walls built up all around us. Then somebody comes along and shows up that it was nothing more than a picket fence, the whole damned time.

But the rust is starting to show on my armour, I've been in this fight for too long. Yet All I can see, is a thousand more wars, coming for You, Coming for Me. So I fight on, in hopes that they never get past me, in hopes that they never reach you.

B U L L E T

By Christopher Whitney

My Heart is the Moon,

Beating pale blue against a backdrop of darkness.

My Soul is a Forest,

Wild, free, and full of undiscovered creatures of nature.

My Pain is an Ocean,

Created from the storms of tears I have cried.

My Love is a Bullet,

Fired down the barrel of a rusty gun.

I feel too much of you,

flowing through me like sapphire water,

and ruby kisses.

We are one, You and I,

two pieces of the same cloth,

two flames of the same fire.

Sanguine

By Christopher Whitney

When I am hurt by love,

something happens to me,

the thunder inside turns to lightning,

and I am never quite the same.

My heart doesn't beat quite like it used to,

every now and then it falters in its rhythm,

and my stomach gets sick.

But my soul,

Wow, my poor beaten soul,

it becomes so close to death,

intimate.

They share sanguine conversation in purgatory,

Like the English share tea and biscuits.

She

She can't be seen by the eyes of boys who have yet to become Men. They will be unable to look beyond the shell of her glorious body and see the kaleidoscope of lights that glisten inside of her. She is not for the weak, and she is not for the cowardly. You are going to have to be willing to bleed a million shades of Love in order to grasp a heart as sharp edged as Hers.

She is terrifying and fierce, she isn't straightforward and she is impossible to read. She is crazy and lost in madness, with the sweet aroma of insanity. She often says a thousand words without making a sound. She has her flaws, and she has her imperfections, but that is okay.

She will fall a lot.

She will be down. A lot.

But she always gets back up. Always. She is unstoppable in her own way. She takes what she wants with passionate abandon, and if it shall cut her hand, she will reach out and take it with the other.

She is not made from blood and bones like the rest of us. She has the stars of the universe inside of her, and that comes complete with a few black holes too.

She is the storm of a century, locked away in the stillness of a minute.

"You have stolen the heart from inside of Me. You have taken everything that I could have been. I can feel the walls crumbling down all around. I have never felt so exposed as a volley of arrows block out the moon. You used to be my shield, now you are the bow."

Christopher Whitney

THE OLD TEDDY BEAR

The old teddy bear, tattered and torn. Once was loved and now is forsaken.

It's stitching is loose and an eye is gone.

But there it sits on the winter's path, left behind in the wake of transition.

The fluff inside is starting to soil, the elements of the world are not being kind.

The old teddy bear, tattered and torn, it will love in the forgotten, and be forgotten in the love.

THE SMOKE

By Christopher Whitney

I dreamed a dream of blackened skies and scorched earth. I saw the clouds on fire and I held out my arms to let the flames of your love pour into me.

I wake to deafening screams that only I can hear. My soul is trying to claw out of my chest, smouldering my heart as it tries to get back to the dream.

I am but the charred ruins of feelings that you had no right to give me.

I am trampled and I am defeated.

I am the smoke you left behind when you burned it all.

THROW ME TO THE WOLVES.

I stand in the pouring rain, hammering on your door. The wolves are snapping at my heels, they try to drag me into the dark. But my fists, they keep on pounding, as I try and get through to You. Can you not hear me calling out your name?

You are hiding on the other side of the door, fingers grasping that deadbolt lock, you keep it nice and steady, and will not let me in. do you not care that my heart bleeds for you?

So you have thrown me to the wolves, but I will dominate this pack, and when I come back this way, will you be the predator, or the prey?

TOO DARK, TOO SCARY.

By Christopher Whitney

TOO DARK YOU SAY,

I SAY THAT IS JUST THE COLOUR OF MY SOUL.

TOO SCARY YOU SAY,

I SAY THAT THEY ARE JUST MY DEMONS.

I HAVE NEVER BEEN ONE TO STAY IN THE SHADOWS,

NOT WHEN THE LIGHT HAS SO MUCH MORE TO OFFER.

I HAVE TOO MUCH IN ME TO EVER TAME IT NOW.

I AM A WOLF. HOWLING FOR MY PACK,

AND IF YOU LISTEN CAREFULLY, SOMEWHERE OUT THERE, BEYOND THE HORIZON, YOU CAN HEAR THEM HOWLING BACK AT ME.

Authors Note: This next one is a favourite piece of mine simply because of the depth in which my words came from. I really felt like this was not just me, making up words. I felt like I could hear this, or feel this, deep in my soul and it just had to be written.

"To the winter born fires I go, stepping on frozen glass along the way. Feeling the clothes falling from my skin, lost into the abyss of strangers and flesh. Tears are falling, into the avenue of history, making memories and puddles along the road. To the winter born fires I go, stepping on pieces of me along the way."

Authors Note: I wrote this next one after somebody told me that writing is free and does not cost anything.

WRITING ISN'T FREE

It costs a great many things.

It costs all the blood that must be put inside the pen in order to release the tender secrets of poetry.

It costs the courage to confess feelings and emotions that are hidden deep within the crooked core of your soul.

It costs the pain that comes with reopening wounds in order for you to write about what haunt the shadows of your eyes.

If you look at writing and see it as "free" then you aren't looking beyond the surface, or the words.

The Soul Wolf

By Christopher Whitney

There is a wolf inside of Me, it lives within the crack along the edge of my soul.

When you walked into my life, it picked up your scent and it thought you might be worthy of the hunt.

It began to venture out of the shadows.

It soon discovered that you were not the one,

You were the hunter, the monster, the liar, and the cheat.

You made me your prey, you ripped me apart and tore open my bones. You destroyed me from the inside.

The wolf saw you, and all the cruelty you unleashed, it backed deeper into that crack along the edge of my soul, making sure that it can never be found.

So that nobody could ever find it. So that nobody could ever do to it,

what you had done to me.

Authors Note: Remember the Haiku Style Poetry that I showed you earlier? The one with the syllable rule of 5,7,5? Well here is my second attempt at this style of poetry.

WILL IT CLOSE

By Christopher Whitney

Cannot stop this heart

As the pain falls all on me

In waves of cold rain

My soul is empty

Gone to the sea of sorrows

Never to return

Your ghost is still there

Standing over my shoulder

With each choice I make

I am torn by love

my wound is still wide open

Never will it close.

WILD HORSES

By Christopher Whitney

The lonely whispers are here. The shadows creep upon me. The wild horses are galloping through me. I wish you had stayed, I dream you are still by my side. I look in the mirror and I want to scream.

I see him some times, the other Me. He's riding on the back of a chestnut stallion. He wants to get to you, he thinks I have lassoed a noose around his throat. He thinks it is I who stops him. But that was never the truth. Because I never held it in. I never held back. I let my emotions pour out of me and into your hands with raw honesty. It was the purest of all the loves that ever lived inside of me. A stampede of mounts traverse the ridges of my thoughts, in search of You. For you are everywhere, even whilst nowhere to be seen. I wish you would shine a light, to show me where you are hiding, to show me the way to go home.

I've been on my own for too long. Without You. I am walking in drunken circles. My steed has closed it's eyes and has given up. But I can't do the same, and I know I am going to have to abandon him. Put him out of his misery and go forward on bloodied feet. Alone.

But I just wish that you would stop me, before I slaughter the entire stable of wild horses that live inside of me, all just to keep my love for you alive.

YOUR DEMONS

I looked into your eyes,

and I saw your demons.

The problem was,

they didn't look scary,

but they did look scared.

It was then that I knew,

You were never trapped with your demons,

They were the ones who were trapped with You.

Christopher Whitney

.Whiskey.

I fill my bed with warm bodies and lonely hearts. I take women like I take my whiskey,

Straight Up,

And Down in One.

They are always gone by morning, my soul is always left feeling cold. I'm not myself any more. I used to be different than this. I feel watered down and you were always my whiskey in a teacup.

But now I drink from the bottle.

I have faded into the background of my own life and now my walls have sharp edges to cut the hands of anyone who tries to pull me back and away from the ledge.

I fill my bed with faceless women that are more a symbol than a soul. A vessel for me to pour myself into for just the one night.

A moment to be bold and unapologetic.

To be wild and reckless.

To be primal and feral.

I touch them with the love I wished that you would give me.

I kiss them with the way I wish you needed me.

I make love to them like they are the last thing on my mind every night before I go to sleep.

I search for You,

in all of them,

I never find you, I never will,

My little Whiskey, in a teacup.

By Christopher Whitney

PART FIVE
S H O C K

"*My body is just a tomb where my heart is buried. My soul is just an empty house, where love used to live.*"

Leave Me Alone. *Don't Leave Me Alone.* Leave Me Alone. Leave Me Alone. Leave Me Alone. Leave Me Alone. Leave Me Alone. Leave Me Alone. **Don't Leave Me Alone.** Leave Me Alone. Leave Me Alone. Leave Me Alone. Leave Me Alone. Leave Me Alone. <u>Don't Leave Me Alone.</u> Leave Me Alone.

Fighting To Make You See Me

By Christopher Whitney

So this is what it feels like,

to be the one who has loved and lost.

A love that can never be saved.

I love you too much to let you go.

But I know that I must.

Still,

How am I to say goodbye to the one I am still madly in love with.

Maybe I am selfish for wanting to keep you, when you don't want to be kept.

I shouldn't be fighting to make you see me.

I drink myself to death every night since you left.

It stops me from begging you to come back.

But I need to let you go,

Because my love for you is selfless.

And your actions tell me that you can only be happy,

With the absence of me.

The Ramblings of Me

She did all that she did because she felt that she did not deserve me. But that is no excuse for hurting people who love you and just want to take care of You. She chose not to love me any more, because she felt that I deserved better. Because of her, I learned to believe in miracles and soul mates.

But because of her,

I also learned that the soul can die, long before the body does. I learned not to put my trust into other people because they will always let you down. Most importantly, I discovered that the people you love, can destroy you the most.

All that you left behind

By Christopher Whitney

I wonder if you ever think about what exactly you left behind.

A best friend. A team mate. A partner. A lover. And a soulmate.

You left behind somebody who chose you over every other person on this planet.

You left behind beautiful memories, golden futures, and incredible dreams.

You left behind sleepy kisses every morning, and hungry kisses every night.

You left behind the eyes that saw you the clearest,

and hands that worshipped you so feverishly.

You left behind a life of happiness,

and stories that would be told for years to come.

You left behind, so much of it and not enough.

But most of all,

You left behind,

ME.

Stubborn Fool

My heart doesn't have a back up plan,

Don't you see that?

You stubborn fool.

If it isn't You.

It's nobody.

It's no one else.

It's Nothing.

Come Home

It was like he had left his body and was an apparition,

Haunting a life that was once his.

And every once in a while, he can hear that voice,

The Rest of Him,

Calling Out,

Come Home... Come Home...

The Darkness sitting next to it

You think you know me.

You tell me that you see me.

But your eyes are off to the side.

You are looking at the light.

And I have always been the darkness sitting next to it.

Either or Neither

By Christopher Whitney

Either it is Yes or No.

Or it is Neither.

I will not let your maybes,

haunt my sleepless nights again.

You are either Mine, and All of Mine,

Or not at all.

You open your heart to Me,

Or I close my door to You.

There are no half measures,

There are no Maybes.

No Trying.

You will or you won't.

I believe only in certainty.

EXPLANATIONS

By Christopher Whitney

As I matured in life, and gained new experiences, I learned not to explain myself to others. It gives them the false belief that they are entitled to know everything you do and you end up justifying yourself to people that have no place to judge you in the first place. But when it came to Her, I told her everything. And I mean EVERYTHING. I explained EVERYTHING. I discussed EVERYTHING. I confessed EVERYTHING. I became an open book and let her fingers trace the Braille of all my secrets.

She would always tell me that I didn't need to explain myself to her. I should have realised it back then, that she was not ready for me. We were not on the same wavelength.

She was so used to boys and their games. Children and their secrets. Cheaters and their lies. It was all that she knew. So she could not see the Real Man standing in front of her.

I never explained anything to her out of obligation. I did it out of desire, to share my world with her. To communicate and build our relationship upon a foundation of trust and honesty. I wanted to share everything, because we were supposed to be a team and I was willing to sacrifice privacy in order to please her unspoken insecurities.

I made changes in my life, and inside of me, to benefit her. I did it all, for her. And I hope that one day, she will stop seeing boys, and start seeing men. I hope that one day, she will stop seeing them, and start seeing Me.

The Colours of the Sky

By Christopher Whitney

What we had, has faded to a quiet whisper that is now lost in the wind.

Once a blazing fire, now a simmering ember.

Once a star, now a black hole.

A Dark Space Where Our Love Used To Be

You drowned me in your dark waters after promising to help me swim. What we once had was terrifying, and it was dangerous. It swallowed all of me and I began to decay on the inside.

But it's not over. It's not too late. Let's do it again, and do it right.

This Love is Killing Me

But we have wasted so much time. My life, with you in it, means everything. And I can't just throw that away. The love is fading but it is still there. Let us change the colours of the sky. Turn them from black to blue, or even green for all I care, as long as it is with you.

Our Love isn't Gone. It's Just Lost.

Authors Note: This was a letter I once wrote amidst the drowning emotion of shock. The person it was for, never read it. But I did, a thousand times over.

Dear You,

Every path I take, all the roads lead back, to this place I cannot go. I stand behind the barrier you have built up and I watch you. I know everything about you and yet it makes no difference to any of this. I could walk away now, again and again, but I would always end up back here in front of you, wishing you could open your eyes and see me. You are where I belong. It calls to me, Your Soul. Every time you tell me to go away, your fragile heart whispers for me to stay. And the more you stand defiant against us, the louder I hear the screams of your spirit. You've locked her away, deep down inside of You, behind a closed door that you bolted, locked, and threw away the key. I love you, I do, with every fibre of me, but that doesn't mean I will stand by and just blindly let you destroy yourself simply because you tell me it is what you want. You know that I know better, I see the parts of you that you hide from yourself. I see beyond the masks as though they are more like open windows. I don't just see the rainbows that you paint, I see the entire spectrum of colours that shimmer within the darkness that swallows You.

You have put me behind the barriers because you believe I should have walked away by now. And I have tried to do exactly that, we both know it. I have tried to walk away every time you threw me away. But it is a ghost world out there, I touch things, and I don't feel. I eat and I cannot taste. There is no light at the end of my tunnel. There is Just You. And every tunnel is just another path I walk to you, because you are not just my True North. You are my Eastern Hills. My Southern Shores. My Western Wonderland. You are not just the compass, you are the arrow and I will do whatever it takes to be the wind that pours between your feathers and gives you flight to fly true.

This is Me. Here I Am, I just want you to let me come inside, this world sucks and I have been waiting for you for so long now. You think this is the end, but I see only the beginning, every time I come back around to your door step. I stand on the corner of this street and the Gods rain down on me, but here I am, watching over you from the shadows.

There is beauty beyond your glimpse, bat your lashes and blink away the fog that has taken you from me. Tell your heart that I am on my way and tell your soul that you will not be afraid any more. Find some courage, because not the hell, nor the pain will change my mind, there is nowhere I would rather be, than with you.

I never saw you coming, but you did and nobody has ever come this far. If I can't have you, I don't want anybody. So I won't quit.

Not on You.

Not on Us.

PART SIX

A COLD REALITY

"The pain I feel within the depths of my soul, will never again, come to light up the night"

Complete Strangers

We Aren't Anything.

You don't Know Me.

You Don't See Me.

Not Any More.

We Are Just Complete Strangers.

Who Happen To Love Each Other.

Open your eyes and tell me what you see,

Am I the forgotten?

Please say that you remember me.

I know that you are there,

Somewhere deep inside.

Am I there too?

Somewhere with you?

Because I am not here,

Not any more.

Silence

By Christopher Whitney

You think this is silence?

I can hear you loud and clear.

I am not worth it.

The battles you must face, the choices you must make,

I am not worth them.

That is what your actions tell me,

And you didn't have to say to a word.

You think your silence allows you to escape without consequence. You believe that if you say nothing, you can avoid accountability. But I have never heard you say so much, as you do when you say nothing at all.

WAR TORN PATH

I just need to tell you, that I know you are going to be death of me. I know your love will kill me, and I know the path I must walk for you is one that will cut my feet, with blistering winds that batter my face.

But it is okay, I am not trying to survive it.

Not any more.

Here I am, and here is my life, take it if you need to.

I give it freely if that is the price I must pay for you.

There is nothing I would not endure, Nothing I would not do,

to keep my place,

Here on this war torn path to You.

.GHOSTS & MIRRORS.

She stands quietly in front of the bathroom mirror, staring sadly at the shadows around her eyes... "I'm Over Him" … She whispers to herself.

The light flickers and the Ghost of Him drifts through the shadows with a predatory gait... "is that what you think, little one?" … He says as his ghostly memory moves up behind her and claims her with a possessive wrap of his arms.

The lights stop flickering, returning to normal and the Ghost of Him is gone, but as she checks her lipstick, and heads on out the door, She could have sworn she heard the smug laughter of Him.

The Island

My Nostrils Flared, And I inhaled the smoke.

But it wasn't burnt wood, or fabric I could smell.

It was something much harder on the soul.

The scent of dreams, simmering to nothing,

Like the sizzle of water, on a hot plate.

My mind is a desolate island,

And my heart, is a shipwreck,

Upon it's black and sandy shore.

Some nights I can't sleep

By Christopher Whitney

When the hour grows late and my mind begins to settle, it is always consumed by the tormenting thoughts of you and how life would improve so much simply by having you at my side.

As the world falls asleep,

I lie awake in discomfort, an ache deep inside my ribcage that I cannot turn off. It is something I cannot name, but I know that it calls for you.

I close my eyes in the dead of night,

And know that nobody will ever understand exactly what you meant to me,

including You.

I rest in silence,

But know that there is always something to be said in the moments when I cannot find the strength to speak. Nobody could ever understand the amount of love that I have inside of Me, all of it, For You. If they did, nobody would ever tell you to walk away from it.

Nobody would ever let You.

And that is what keeps me awake at night, it is not the losing you. It is the knowledge that if only you would have just fucking tried, I would have shown you that I was worth the bloody fight.

Some nights, I can't sleep,

Because there is nothing next to me. More than anything, I want to feel close to somebody again. I want to remember how it felt,

To Not Feel Alone.

Do You Think?

"Maybe people don't really change, they just eventually stop pretending to be somebody they are not, and have never really been."

I Am

I am a shattered lamp.

Knocked from a side table by the careless steps of a loveless lover.

I am something that once was,

but isn't any more.

Like the fading of paint upon a worn down fence.

I need some time away, from myself.

I need a holiday, where I can be somebody else.

Just for one day,

I want to be free.

Free from Me.

PART SEVEN

P A I N

"... The fire in his soul flickered beneath the onslaught of a cold wind that tore through him, and within a blink, the flames were snuffed and he spiralled into darkness. ..."

BROKEN DREAMS

He walks a life of broken dreams,

He sees a world as void of life,

as he is void of her.

He is bitter in the end,

Because people around him,

They laugh and smile,

And all he does is hurt.

Never Knew

"I am constantly amazed as I stand there, torn apart and ripped open. And I see pieces of myself in their hands that I never knew existed within Me."

A Word to The Wounded

They will never understand, what they did to us. The sheer depth of pain that they put our hearts through. The toxic and corrosive damage that they leave behind. Their lies, and their betrayals ruin us. They shatter us and broke us in ways that will never really heal. They cause permanent destruction to our heart, and our soul. And They Will Never Understand That

Because if they did, how could they be okay with the way they treat us? I could never do any of this to her. It would ruin me. I wouldn't be able to hurt her as easily as she hurt me. But they don't care what wreckage they leave us in. And they are not blind to it, they know it will hurt us, and they choose to do it anyway. And we continue to tell our souls and our stupid hearts that we need to let go of all this pain that they have forced down our throats. But neither our souls, nor our hearts, will listen. They are too afraid of the possibility that letting go of all this consuming pain inside of us, means letting go of them too. And it is so hard, to be us, and know that even as they cut us down, our own hearts will make excuses for them. And our own fucking soul,

Chooses them, Over Us, Every. Single. Time.

As Good As Any

By Christopher Whitney

I know, as good as any, what it is like to be haunted by heartbreak that never goes away. To be caught up in a life which I can find no meaning.

I know, as good as any, what it is like to be a lost whimper within the sounds of the sea. To be hollowed out by ruthless words that echo for an eternity after they are spoken.

I know, as good as any, what it is like to pretend you are okay when everything is falling apart. To put on a smile when all you want to do is break down and cry.

I know, as good as any, what it is like to hear pain within every song that sings. To see hurt in every movie that plays and feel bitterness in everything growing around you.

I know, as good as any, what it is like to have somebody tell you they love you, whilst they give that same love to another, every night of your life.

I know, as good as any, what it is like to feel completely, and utterly, alone. To be hanging on to the edge, whilst everyone around you is trampling on your fingers.

She Crucified Me.

I was the one who let her in, when she walked through all of my walls and knocked on the door. I was the one who was there for her, through ill health and low times. Through the thick and the thin of it all.

I was the one that stood against the blistering heat of her scorch mouthed demons, and stayed.

But when the chips were down, and the tables turned,

She Crucified Me.

And she did it for Him.

And that is what really kills Me.

DEAD MEMORIES

By Christopher Whitney

There is a certain tragedy in losing the one you love.

It is not just your heart that dies in fractured torment.

It is not just your soul, that bleeds away.

It is when the memories begin to die, that tragic things are lost.

Memories that will never come to be.

Memories that began as hopes and fantasies, and will never come to fruition.

Memories that you once saw as the future.

Now you watch them pass on by, unborn.

I think that is why I miss you so much.

I didn't know that those hopes were our unborn treasures,

That they would be stillborn and become a graveyard of dead memories.

I am a devil out of hell,

a sinner who sinned for you.

And that's the thing, isn't it?

I didn't just give you my heart,

Nor just my soul.

I gave you all my sins too,

Because I wanted to be damned,

Just to live in the night with you.

I bleed from cuts that hide beneath the flesh,

and stab myself in the heart,

for a fool that will never love me.

Not Thrice

When you are going through heartbreak, people like to tell you that what doesn't kill you, makes you stronger.

Well it DID kill me.

Not Once, Not Twice, And Not Thrice.

It killed me a hundred times over and it still does.

I died every time I saw her with him, I died every time I lay in bed at night, knowing she was in bed with him.

I died every single morning that I woke up and found that empty space beside Me.

It didn't make me stronger,

I just got used to Dying.

Justification

I have been justifying it.

Justifying You.

It hurts Me.

But I always try to justify it on your part.

Because I am protective.

Of You.

Not my heart or my feelings.

Me and My Pain

I'm still where you left me, I kept that promise when I said that I Won't Move. My heart still beats your name and my soul still weeps for you. I have only one direction in me, and it always takes me towards You.

I'm still in love, it never fades, and it never forgets.

I am in love with the memories and the ghosts.

My pain is very lonely, as I slowly die inside.

I'm becoming too weak to speak about it.

Confined to fake smiles that I can barely muster,

And so many "I'm Fine" responses making my voice hoarse.

I'm learning to be silent, and still, and to suffer on my own.

To be alone together,

Me and My Pain.

Christopher Whitney

World of Excuses

"Perhaps you would be able to better yourself by learning from all of your disastrous mistakes. But you can only do that when you first stop denying them and pushing them into the world of excuses."

Every Step of the Way

Wanting to feel love from somebody who doesn't want to love you is a very painful addiction. It will blacken your heart, as it cracks, shrivels, and dies. It puts holes in it so that the pain can pour out of You. Like a rusty bucket with one too many bullet holes in it. It will kill your soul. And you will actually feel it dying inside of you, every step of the way.

Authors Note: Remember that unpublished novel I once told you about, back in the earlier pages of this book? Well here is another piece from that, it is from a chapter that I wrote when drowning in pain.

"I am Fine." I said, a little too sharply. And she saw it before I could hide it. A gentle frown creased her brow. She crossed the path towards me and I thought she was about to ask me questions. About things that I knew I couldn't talk about. Those answers would come with tears and I didn't want her; or anyone, to see me weak like that. But she didn't ask any questions, she didn't say anything. She just sat down beside me on the bench and we spent the next hour watching the stars. Saying everything, whilst saying nothing at all.

-From "The Price of Souls" The Novel I never released.

PART EIGHT

H U R T

"I have a valley of dreams in my heart, but all the flowers are dying, and all of the nightmares are waking up."

NOT AT ALL

By Christopher Whitney

All I know is that when you are not here, everything hurts more than it ever should be able to.

It hurts the way I miss you, with every sound and syllable that seems to know your name. The way every colour and shape seems to tell a story about one of our memories.

It hurts the way I'm lonely, no matter how many others I surround myself with. It hurts the way I cannot smile, or enjoy the company of other people because their happiness reminds me that I am not happy, not even a little, not at all.

It hurts the way I yearn for you. Pining all day through. I mourn a ghost that is yours and grieve for a love that was never really mine.

It hurts the way you are not mine to miss. The way my loneliness is not your problem. The way my yearning is unnoticed and I am as forgettable as I am forgotten.

It hurts the way you do not hurt, not even a little, not at all.

Ravenous Black

Can we just see each other?

One Last Time.

I promise, after that, I will let you go free.

I see now that you were never meant for me. But I just need you to need me,

One Last Time.

I need a taste of what it was like when you still loved me, I can pretend, or at least, I can pretend to pretend.

Maybe I don't deserve it,

But the heart wants what it wants. So come and move closer, in my direction. You are the Queen to my King and I just want to claim the throne one more time.

I want to be your king again, just for tonight.

Because you are the only star that ever sparkled in the ravenous black of my nights.

OPENLY CLOSED

By Christopher Whitney

I close my eyes and I think of You.

I cannot tell you how it makes me feel,

to see you sitting against the back of my eyelids,

smiling back at Me.

I cannot describe how I envision you there,

and let my mind trace the shadows of your mouth.

I take a deep breath,

I open my eyes,

And I feel that goodbye kiss on my lashes.

The pain changes you. We pretend it is not happening, but it does. It becomes your nature to trust less, and suspect more. You become an over thinker and over analyser. You develop self sabotaging habits and become somewhat of an introvert. You shut people out at every turn because pain changes You. You don't ever want to go through that bitter and world destroying pain again so you evolved. First You Break. Then You Survive. Then you come back. But never as the same person. THAT person died with the love.

THE THREE DAYS

By Christopher Whitney

I am so disorderly. Demented and befuddled. Some days I feel like my love for you has decayed to nothing, and all that lingers are phantoms of what I once felt for you. Some times I don't yearn for you and I don't feel quite as deflated. I start to blame you for allowing our love to disintegrate beneath the venom of all your wickedness. On those days, I feel content to watch you fade away. I tell myself that it is okay because if you don't want me, then you don't deserve me anyway. I tell myself that you were never real, and it was all just a game of chase. You had the power to make my dreams come true. All you had to do was love me like you promised you always would. But you didn't, that was your loss and so I tell myself that you are beneath me. Just another heart breaker who won't get the best of me. I feel stronger on those days. Better off without You.

Then there are the days where I am caught up in a tempestuous state of existence. Self pity and over emotional thoughts are my only friends on those days. I feel like it was all my fault because I am not worth the love. I tell myself that you did mean all of those love stories you built around me when you fought to break down all of my walls. I tell myself that when I finally yielded to you, and let you inside, you saw the real me and realized I was not worth loving. You discovered that I am unlovable.

And finally, there are those days where I just miss you. The most frequent of all the days, and the hardest. On those days I think of you at every sunrise, hoping that it is the day you will come back to me. I count the chapters of my life that have passed by since you left me and I try not to panic. I am running out of chapters and if you don't come back. You will miss them all. I will be forced to live my final chapter without you.

And what a sad ending it will be.

If you never come home to Me.

Tsunami

The answer to what we could have been,

now sits at the bottom of the ocean.

In the same place you left me to drown

forever in the tsunami of your betrayal.

Words Said

The words that hurt my guts.

You said them all.

All that could have been said to cut, scar, and break,

All of them, fell from your tongue.

You left me behind with them.

When you said those words, my world shattered.

Every time I think of those words, that shattered world crashes into me like a meteor shower.

It leaves me cold and out of breath.

Burnt and Broken.

You are Never Coming Home.

Never. Coming. Home.

It is the end of the World,

And You are the last thing I can see.

B U R I E D

You turn away from me,

and you won't listen to the things I have to say.

And the sight of your back murders all the words in my throat,

replacing them with thorns that silence me to death.

I reach out to grasp your shoulder,

but you take a step forward,

away from me and into the embrace of his arms.

You fade from sight and my heart falls out of my chest,

shattering against the cobbles of the road we had built together.

You took with you my blood, to use as mortar on the new road,

that you build with him, and I am left here,

to become overgrown with nettles, and wilderness.

Buried by your absence.

After all that we have been through,

I will never forget You.

And after all this is said and done,

You are still the one,

The one my soul whispers to,

when my heart is too sad to beat.

You were different, and it was as though I was seeing the real you for the first time in all the years we knew each other.

I saw that we could never go back to how we were before,

because I didn't love you, I loved who I thought you were,

I loved the person you pretended to be in order to win my heart. And that is how I managed to get over you.

The Realisation that I was in love with the memories,

in love with a ghost,

in love with somebody who never existed.

You left me,

but you took pieces of me with you.

The pieces that I gave to you,

to fix you and make you whole again.

You left me broken so that you could repair yourself.

Then you gave those pieces to somebody else.

You broke me, to build Him into somebody you could love.

I will go. But I will think of you, every second that passes after here.

I will love you in my heart for the rest of my days and even though you have turned your back on me, and sent me away to walk the rest of this path on my own, it changes nothing for me. The memories are painful as I think about what we once had, and now those memories are all I have to take with me as you go off into the night, because we both know now, that I am not what you want, or need. And I hate that about myself, the realisation that I will just never be good enough, to be the one for You.

I wish you well, I hope that you find all you dream of searching for.

And I wish you Love.

I wish you Love.

Forever and a Day.

And all the days after that.

PART NINE
LOVE

"I didn't watch where I was going, and I have fallen into You."

As Well As Time

You always left for work before me, so your alarm always went off first, but I would make sure to wake up too. Some times I would lure you back to bed, to quench my wicked thirst in the entanglement of your limbs. But other times I would just watch you, and quietly fall in love as you sat there getting ready for work. Perhaps you thought me crazy, for doing such a thing. But I thought you were crazy, for thinking I could ever miss such beautifully raw opportunities. Because you were always the sunshine in my life, and who would not wish to watch their sun, rise every morning?

Maybe love is just acceptance, as you are, and who you are. Maybe love is just about seeing all the bad in each other and saying … "I accept that, and I love you any way" … I don't have the answer to everything and some times "Maybe" is the best kind of certainty I can muster. What I do know is that you leave me feeling hopeful, that not all is Lost in Me.

It is just how I see you, differently.

I once asked you if you knew that for the first few minutes of the day, you could watch the sun and it wouldn't hurt your eyes. What I never told you, was that if it hurt my eyes to see your face, I would spend the last few minutes before going blind.. looking right at You.

I just would.

And after I was blind, I would simply smile. Because you were the last thing I saw and your vision was forever imprinted in my eyes. As you have always been, since the first moment I saw You,

And my heart stood still, as well as time.

Into Mine

Whatever it is that you think of yourself,

You cut through my darkness like a ray of the brightest colours.

And there is no way,

That I am leaving this world,

without the taste of your lips,

Burned into Mine.

My Night Sky

You are My night sky, I think you would feel like a unique canvass beneath my finger tips.

You could be Mine, and I could be Yours.

I think you would paint something lovely.

I think I would write poetry along your every curve,

Draw miracles into the shadows of your scars,

And paint your soul with the colours of many things.

Until "All black" was merely a back drop,

to something much more fluorescent.

I could be your breath, filling your lungs,

with the intoxication of all,

That I would do to You.

HE

He can still taste her sins, on the tip of his tongue.

He can still feel her warmth, rising to the touch of his fingers.

He can still hear her love, whimpering against his earlobe.

CLIMAX

By Christopher Whitney

Come lay down beside me, let my fingers leave whispered delights along the curve of your hips.

Let my lips trace a path across your ribs.

Let my breath wash down your spine with the gasping growl of desire.

Let me reach across to You, and pull you close to me.

Let me take you in my arms. Possessively and with intent. Let me kiss awake your fire, that will warm you down to the clutch of your thighs.

Come lay down beside me, and let me fall in love with every inch of You, As you take every inch of me.

Let me drive you to the edge with a thundering clash of bodies, and we will ride that storm together, as we spiral into climax.

Come lay down beside me, and let me wake up next to you in the morning,

And every Morning After that

Divinely

Pour some of that sexiness on Me.

Let me drown in you.

Sticky hunger, and warm like butter.

Give yourself to Me,

And I will build cities inside of you.

I will show you a whole universe hidden,

between the pixels of your flesh.

I will show you, what a man like me,

Can do to a woman,

As divinely delicious as You.

My Wants

I don't just want your heart, I want your soul too. I want your mind, and I want your body. I want it all. I don't just want to love you, I want to own you, claim you, and possess You. I want to dominate you when you have been a good girl, and punish you when you've been bad.

I don't just want to smother you in kisses, I want my bruises to creep up your hips and around your wrists from holding you too tightly, too roughly. I want to steal your breath away and make you beg for more.

I don't just want you on your feet at my side, I want you on your knees in front of me too.

I want your submission and your surrender.

I don't just want to show you what real love is like, I want to show you what real hunger is like, when it is scorching across your pretty mouth and trickling down between your trembling thighs. I want to sink my claws into the meat of you and drag you close enough to hear the sadistic sigh that breathes out of my mouth when I look at You. I want to show you the difference, between everybody else,

And Me.

DOMINATION

I'm not here to play games,

I am not here to take part,

I'm not here to come second,

And I am certainly not here to quit.

I am here to Dominate,

I am here to fly,

I am here to win your heart,

And you can just watch me try.

I CHOOSE YOU, BECAUSE I CHOOSE ME

By Christopher Whitney

Even when I must sacrifice myself to do so, I will always choose You. And before you walk out of that door, I will tell you why choosing you is an easy choice for me. Then you can run, and stay blissfully ignorant to the fact that you always run from your fears.

My life, has no meaning, if you are not in it.

There is no life without you, not for this man.

So I choose you, because I choose me.

I choose Life, and that is You. Nothing will change that. Whether it is a life as your lover, friend, or somebody you never speak to again, it still won't change the fact that when I wonder what the meaning of life is,

You are Always my answer.

It is my truth.

And that is why, you belong to Me.

Because nobody... and I mean nobody... will ever see you the way I do.

Because they are not looking through the eyes of your soulmate,

They are not looking through the eyes of me.

HALO

Darkness shrouds the edges of my halo.

As crooked as it sits,

Against my twisted horns,

You cannot take me,

or grasp on my thorns.

For a beast has taken claim of this heart,

And his possessiveness will slay you,

Before he ever lets us part.

Everlasting Feast

By Christopher Whitney

I like it rough and fierce,

That is just my tastes.

It pleases me that little bit more,

to know that there is a primal, animalistic, desire fuelling every act unfolding in our tangle of flesh.

I like to feel the flush of burning heat,

As it spreads through my body and into yours.

Like a shuddering heatwave.

I like it when it's wrong, but feels so wickedly right.

And I like it when it makes me hungry,

like a ravenous and feral beast,

Looking for You,

My Everlasting Feast.

Perfect Storm

By Christopher Whitney

If you were a book, I would never stop reading, even if it cuts my fingers every time I turn the page.

Because it is You,

And you are the only pain I ever want to feel.

It is not that I enjoy pain, because I don't.

I hate it.

But life isn't always sunshine & rainbows,

And together we make the perfect storm.

I want your thunder, quaking through my bones.

I want your lightning, crackling through your finger tips.

I want the laughter & the tears. The ups & the downs.

I want You, and every chapter, in every story,

That we will ever write together.

BOYS WATCH FAIRY TALES TOO.

WHEN I WAS YOUNG, I WATCHED THEM ALL. BUT I NEVER WANTED TO BE THE PRINCE CHARMING WITH EVERYBODY FALLING AT HIS FEET. CROWDS FLOCKING AROUND HIM TO CONFESS THEIR SHALLOW LOVE THAT COMES A DIME A DOZEN.

I WANT TO BE THE BEAST,

WHO EVERYONE HATES, FEARS, AND SHUNS.

THE BEAST WHO EVERYBODY RUNS AWAY FROM,

SO THAT I CAN LOVE, THE ONE WHO STAYS.

MEN DESERVE FAIRY TALES TOO.

.Forever.

Forever was never about eternity.

It was never about the future.

Forever is now,

And all that we either

Never want to end,

Or wish had never started.

I Never Chose You

By Christopher Whitney

I never chose you because it made sense to do so, because it was expected of me, or because it was the right thing to do. I chose you because loving you made me forget that there was even a choice. The longing for you that I felt was so intense, I finally began to believe in fates, soulmates, and destiny.

And I know, without a slither of a doubt, that no one will ever love you like I do. There are so many things in life that I am uncertain about, but I know that I will love you until the day I die, I know that I will never forget you, and no matter the horrors that I must bare witness to, I will never look away.

My eyes will always search for You.

My heart will always beat for you.

My Soul, will always Find Yours.

Into The Night

By Christopher Whitney

And as I go off into the long cold night, I take with me the knowledge that I have loved you for a thousand lives. And no matter how many times the gods reincarnate me.

New Body.

New Life.

New Heart.

I will still find You.

And I will love you...

...Life, after life, after Life...

One Day

One Day, You will look into my eyes and see that there were never any questions surrounding us,

Only Answers.

And perhaps the answer to everything you will ever want to know, hides away inside of just one kiss.

Watching

She is Like the Moon,

Surrounded by Darkness,

At home with the black of the unknown.

But once it is time for her to rise,

She shines like the sun itself is watching.

My Shooting Star

I call you my shooting star not because I believe you to be a clump of rock that fell from the sky,

You are my shooting star because you are every wish I will ever make.

No matter how far you walk away from me,

No matter how many different stars I see,

Whenever I look upon them with a sad wish in my heart,

It is You I see & wish for,

It is Always You.

Blue Skies

By Christopher Whitney

You are like a beacon in the night sea.

For so long I have been shrouded by the mists of suffering,

Now the fog is starting to fade,

And my vision returns to Me.

They say the sky looks beautiful,

When you finally pass through to the other side of the storm,

But I wouldn't know,

Because since my eyes found you,

I haven't been able to look away.

You Are My Blue Skies

I swear that when my heart beat your name for the first time,

the whole world stopped and listened.

PART TEN
PASSION

"You are never really gone, because you live forever in my heart"

ONE DAY

One Day You Smiled at Me,

And I saw every tomorrow that I had ever wanted to live.

I heard the sound of the heavens within your laughter,

And I saw home in your eyes

One Day You Smiled at Me,

And I fell in love with you, every day after that.

BITE

You think that you know passion, woman?

One night with me and I will redefine everything you thought you knew about the passion of Man

My passion is a feral animal, born to hunt.

It is deep rooted, frighteningly fierce, and as wild as the hurricane that is coming for you.

It is a hunger that claws to get out and fights to be unleashed upon it's prey.

And the only prey I see here,

is You.

So be a good girl, come here now, bare your throat,

And let me just take One. Little. Bite.

It Wouldn't be Nice,

It would be perfect.

Sitting with the love of your life in your arms,

Keeping each other warm, on a cold day.

THAT

is a perfect moment.

The Struggle is Real

Christopher Whitney

Real Love, is a Struggle.

It's fucking Hard.

And anybody who says love is easy,

Has never loved somebody as much as I love You.

Because Real Love,

Never Comes Easy,

The path to it is riddled with challenges,

Fights,

And Trials that you have to go through.

Real Love isn't Easy.

It's just worth it.

You

By Christopher Whitney

All I wanted,

Was to fall in love with your smile for the rest of my days,

And to hold you in my arms for the rest of Yours.

I will always want MORE of You,

But I will never want more THAN You.

I have an itch deep in my soul,

And the only way for me to scratch it,

is by rubbing up against Yours.

The Beast That Watches

Be careful before you mess with her,

There is a beast that watches over her,

from the shadows of her secrets,

And he will swallow you whole,

Before he ever lets the likes of You hurt her.

Poetry

She is the Poetry, I'm just the pen.

And seeing her smile,

it puts the sun into the sky of my life,

A place that has only ever known dark clouds.

Yet

You are Mine.

Your submission will be absolute and in your bones you will feel the melody of every symphony I will carve into your soul.

When I'm done with you...

Well...

There isn't a word for that Yet.

Some times,

After a Long Day,

I need a taste of **whiskey.**

Some times,

After a long day,

I need a taste of **You.**

THE UNIVERSE

The World has a way of coming to life when you are near,

It starts to wake up and blink away it's darkness.

There are signs, and there are warnings,

But my love for you is like a Lion,

And it roars louder than our demons.

For now we are an unfinished story,

The final pages are yet to be written,

Maybe I will never reach the final chapter.

But the universe will always be watching,

Because it believes in us,

Even when we don't believe in ourselves.

Christopher Whitney

A piece by Christopher Whitney

Heaven

The moon lazes, low in the black velvet sky.

A heatwave of chills ripple through the air. Tender breezes kiss upon my sweaty flesh as I unfold into You.

Within You, I watch the night, and all of the stars that bring me to my knees.

I smell the lust, and the scent of the moon that tempts my nature. Wild and savage in all of it's primal glory.

I just want to kiss you. Let the night blow in through the window as I keep you warm. I want to taste every edge of you through your lips. I want to close my eyes, bite your tongue into my mouth and see my future in blazing stars of fiery connection.

I just want to touch You, breathe you in through my finger tips as they explore the darkest parts of You. I want to chain you to Me and unfold you like blooming petals on a summer seasoned rose.

I just want to love you, like it is the last time I ever will. Savour it like you are the only thing in my world. I want to commit great sins upon your flesh and thrust you straight into heaven.

When the sky fell down.

We were two lost souls, You and I.

When there was no time or space, there was only, You and I

Before the light crept in, and the darkness washed it away,

There was always a You,

And there was always an I.

Then all those stars did fall,

From the sparkling mess up above,

And your soul collided with Mine.

Then there was no You,

And there was no I.

Just Us.

Senses

I Sense The Wild Thing In You,

The Beast Of Me Is Calling,

For It To Come Out And Play.

She Belongs With The Wolves,

She Belongs With Me.

A World to Call Home

"I would rather die a thousand deaths with You, than to live for a single second in a world where I don't love you. I will sail the seas of You, on an unsinkable ship. I will search for undiscovered lands inside of You and build a world to call home."

Tree Swing

By Christopher Whitney

I know that I just can't seem to do it right. I cannot love the way society has programmed everybody else around me, to love.

I want to be the wind that cuts through your hair when you sit beneath the summer sun on a crudely made tree swing that I built, just for You.

I want to be that subtle flicker of light that glistens through your eyes whenever you smile.

But I also want to be the spit on your teeth, left behind by the smear of your tongue when something turns you on.

I want to be the rage that snaps & crackles at your finger tips when something makes you angry.

I want to be every thing that moves through your life,

And everything that stands, completely still.

The Passing of Time

By Christopher Whitney

Time Has Passed,

And I have long since accepted the end. But I want you to know that I still miss you, and think of you from time to time. And by that I do not mean once a week, or under every blue moon. I mean every day, and every night, you are in the dark side of my mind.

My mornings are still spent, wishing I could move on, but my evenings are often spent, wishing you would think of me.

I knew that I was hard to love, and it was easier just to walk away like you did. But I also knew that I loved hard, and that often seemed to push you away too.

So time has passed,

But I want you to know,

I love You Now,

And I loved you yesterday,

And every tomorrow to come,

I Will Love You.

PART ELEVEN
SCRAPS OF ME

"And in the end... I will love you forever... and miss you a day more than that."

Author's Note: *Part Ten was originally intended to be the final part of this book, but I was looking through my journals and found one that was more like a scrap book, it had little tiny pieces I had written that did not belong to any poem or larger piece. It was simply a collection of small sentences, and lines, that still manage to bring out the emotions inside of me with such few words needed to do so. So consider this, and any Parts following, a freebie! And enjoy this scrap book collection of pieces!*

...

I shut down and turn everyone away at the door, as though it is a crime to not be You.

...

I can't stop my hands from shaking, as I write about why my heart is breaking.

...

I wanna sit up at 2am with you, eating cereal.

...

I will push you off a cliff with one hand, and hold onto you with the other.

...

My insecurities are laws, issued by a council of demons who live inside my ribcage.

...

Look at You, fading to silence, you must feel so courageous, taking the cowards way out.

...

Even if I could cut out my heart, the rest of me would still find a way to keep on loving her.

...

I was so starved of love, like a forced upon depravity, you came along at a time, when even a knife looked like a kiss.

...

Well, well, well... Look what the devil dragged in.

...

I get so angry with myself when I look back and see all that trust I poured into the hands of people who didn't deserve it.

...

What I want, is to take all this love I have for you, and dissolve it all.

...

A broken heart to me, is not a broken heart to you, so don't look down on me, because I won't look up to You.

…

I dream of dreams that will not be dreams of You.

…

Dreams come true, without You.

…

There is so much left to see, inside this cage of me, but I will always learn, the key will always burn, as I hold it in my hand, and watch it turn to sand.

…

I lean into the embrace of death itself, and it holds me close enough just to keep me alive.

…

I engulfed myself in flames, just so you had a place to get warm.

…

I faded away so quietly that nobody even noticed when I was finally gone.

…

The thorn, it pricks the finger, but the flower is the one who bleeds.

…

There is therapy in this blood that fills my fountain pen.

…

From the broken shards of pain, I grow.

…

If I am not worth the goodnight, You are not worth the goodbye.

…

There is a seed of hate inside of me and it terrifies me how it is starting to take root.

…

The worst enemies I have ever faced, were those who used my heart as their weapon.

…

My heart is a battle tank.

…

The eyes often cannot see what the heart does, but the heart always sees more, than the eyes ever will.

…

This heart of mine will turn to stone, so that it won't hurt, when you leave me alone.

…

He knew well that all it takes is a beguiling smile to hide an injured soul and nobody would ever be able to notice just how broken he really is inside.

…

I want to go back to a time when I am unbroken, I want to go back to the other me, the one who didn't have a hole in the heart.

…

You see that line? The one as thin as a single hair? Where the sky meets the sea? Let's runaway to there.

…

How long must I love you, until you will love me back?

…

If loving you kills me, then take my soul, and take my whole life too.

…

Some times, I whisper your name to myself. Always in quiet or hiding, I whisper it out loud just to hear it again. Just to try and feel you there. I never do.

…

Every once in a while, I find myself wishing for you to love me again, then I remember that you never did in the first place.

…

Find the one who introduces you to others, as their soulmate.

…

In the early hours of the morning, before the sun wakes, or the birds sing, in that neverlasting silence, I hear your name.

…

I am descending into a darkness so intense, it will blind you.

…

We've all got baggage, some of it is heavier than others. But that doesn't mean we can't just stick 'em in the trunk and hit the road on the journey of a lifetime.

…

There is no easy way to let go of you. But holding on to you, is letting go of me.

…

There is life in your eyes. There is life in You.

…

You will always be the love of my life, but you will be my death too.

…

I have learned more from what is missing, than I ever did when you were filling the spaces.

…

I am a lonely mountain, and your echo haunts the misty peak of my soul.

…

She was the kind of girl, who sought answers for questions that never needed to be asked.

…

If I am not here to love you, I am not here at all.

…

I am barely holding on, but at least it is not on to You.

...

Why must my heart be so obstinate? It riots in my chest, protesting my mind, and refusing to unlove You.

...

Everything matters. But nothing matters, quite like You.

...

All nightmares look like dreams, when you take out reality and replace it with hope.

...

Sit on the fence if you want, don't whine when it rots away beneath you.

...

Expressing yourself is the food that feeds the hungry, and you cannot help but offer a meal, when the teeth begin to snap.

...

There is a shadow inside all of us, something wild, that cannot be explained. The light doesn't drown it out. The light embraces it. And so should we.

...

Passion is the fuel to the soul. The more things you are passionate about, the more of the world's beauty you are able to see.

…

I think we are better as strangers, because we were never really anything more.

…

Take off your shoes, walk barefoot in the grass, know that all of your troubles, will one day pass.

…

The tears dry quicker these days.

…

I wonder if I am missed at all in all this thundering silence.

…

I am forever a tragedy of lost love.

…

You shined like the brightest star, but turned out to be nothing more than a trick of the light.

…

Don't try to figure me out. We see things in opposite colours.

…

Pass through the horizon and disappear from my eyes if you wish. But the only end to my world that I see, is the absence of you.

…

I am finally starting to see, that you are poisonous to me.

…

You are my permanent reminder that true evil really does exist.

…

True love is heaven described with a feeling instead of a word.

…

To see a delusion you have carried for so long, finally shatter in front of your eyes, is an unexplainable explanation about the pain you went through in order to carry it in the first place.

…

I am in the most bittersweet, unreturned love with You.

...

Wake me up when going to sleep isn't the only way to stop the pain.

...

We set fire to the world together, then you tossed me into the flames and watched me burn along with it.

...

Keep yours walls up, I don't care. I will still pass you wilted roses through the gaps.

...

I am not a rat in a cage, I am a wolf in a wild forest.

...

This rain, oh how it falls and never stops. Even when the sun is shining, the rain still falls washing away any hope I have of seeing my blue skies again.

...

Her eyes are the most beautiful pits of hell to become lost in.

...

When I see her, my heart gasps in adoration and my soul wakes up from slumber.

When I see her, I see my future hidden away inside dreams and fantasies that will never come to pass.

…

The pain in my heart, is whispering to me again.

Time to remember it says, time to bleed.

…

People say, myself included, that no matter what you must go through or endure, love is worth it. But there is a part of me, whispering in the quiet, and it says: Stand in the ashes of a million broken hearts and ask those dead souls if love was worth it. Their absolute silence is your answer.

…

Lost You. Found Me. Won.

PART TWELVE
QUESTIONS

"Your wings were broken, so I cut off my own. To give them to you, so that you could fly. You put them on, took one look at me. Then you flew far away, and left me for dead."

I get asked a lot of questions everyday on my Facebook page. I answer them as often as I can but I realised that I have never actually done a Q&A session. So I figured why not celebrate the completion of my new book by putting my very first Q&A inside my very first book! These are questions asked by my followers on my official Facebook page. I answered honestly and to the best of my ability, please understand that my answers are personal opinions. I am in no way telling anybody what is right, wrong, best, or worst. I am just sharing, bits of me.

Q: How do you get so deep without going under? - Sheila

You don't. You can't. To get deep, you have to leave the safety of the shallows. You have to go under, beneath the surface, beneath the waves. If you -want- to go deep, you have to -go- deep. I go under every time I write, there is no stopping that. If I didn't, I wouldn't be able to write because I need to feel it. So I do go under, every time, and some times it is hard to come back up again afterwards. I need to recharge, then I get back into the fight and kick arse all the way back to the surface. And the next time I write, I go right back under, and do it all over again. Such is the life of a poet, blood is ink, and pain is beauty.

Q: How do you breathe when even the air suffocates you? - Sharon-Lea

With Breaths. Slow and Deep. The intoxication around you is suffocating your mind, not your lungs, it may feel like it, but that isn't what is happening. And you just have to go through the motions, tell yourself that if you really weren't breathing, you would be dead, but there you are, still alive, so you must be breathing. Bring logic into it, treat it like something to be solved none-spiritually, But intelligently. Go through the motions and fake it if you have to. Eventually, the breathing will get easier. It really is Mind over Matter. If you can't beat it, cheat it. And if you can't cheat it, act dumb and pretend you have won anyway.

Q: How do you know when you are in love? - Sonya

Ask me this question a few years ago and I would have told you that when you are in love, you just know. But I do not believe that any more. You can often think you are in love when you are not, and you can often not see that you are in love, when you are. Some times you can be in love with the memory of somebody but not the present reality of them, and it gets confusing and you end up thinking that you are still in love with that person, but you are not. You just used to be (Because not all love lasts forever, that's soulmate talk.) The only thing I know for certain about being in love is that it can really, really hurt. And it makes you so incredibly vulnerable and if you fall in love with the wrong person, they will quite simply, destroy you. And the kick in the teeth is that usually, when you discover they are the wrong person, it is too late. Because you are already in love. I really don't know any more how you know that you are -really- in love. You just have to wait for your heart to tell you the answer, and you have to be willing to look deep enough to find that answer sometimes because it can be barely more than a whisper... Ask yourself this, Would you sacrifice yourself for them? Really think about it, don't just claim that you would and not know for certain. If you had to put a gun to your own head right now and squeeze the trigger so that they could live, not with you, but with somebody else, who they will love for the rest of their life, would you pull the trigger? Because if you really would, then you are probably in love, but if you wouldn't. You definitely are not truly, in love. In my opinion.

Q: Where does your writing come from? What is your writing process? - Thomas

My writing comes from pain. It comes from my heart, my mind, and my soul. It is a cocktail of emotions that I try to put words to. My writing comes from love, and heartbreak, and sadness. It comes from depression, suicidal feelings, and destruction. My writing comes from all of me, every bone, fibre, and drop of blood. It all has a part in my work. My process is usually simple. I sit down, late at night when the world is at its quietest, I pour myself a drink of whiskey (or make a cup of tea) and I just start writing. Some times I keep the silence, and some times I break it with music.

But There is nothing special about my process, I just decide I want to bleed, and instead of cutting myself with a knife, I pick up a pen and cut myself with words.

Q: What is the first book that made you cry? What is the first book that made you love books? What is your favourite book? What book are you reading right now? - Alex

The first book that made me cry took me a while to remember because I must admit, I don't cry a lot over a book. Though there is one time, I was young and I read a book called 'Moses Beech' by Ian Strachan. I only ever read it that one time and I don't remember all of it because it was that long ago. But I do recall that I actually stole the book, from a library (Sorry!) during a difficult time in my teen years. I read it in a few days and when I finished and closed it, I was lying on my bed thinking about it and I cried at the melancholy ending. It was not sobbing or anything full on emotional, it was a few silent tears, but that's the only time a book has moved me to tears. (And yes, if you are curious, I returned the book. Mailed it to them actually LOL) The first book that made me love books? Again, this is a tough one. I always liked reading but I guess that the one that really made me appreciate books was one called 'The Runaways' by Ruth Thomas. My English teacher in high school made me read it as part of a project. I loved that book and read it back to back about four times. The characters, the story, the journey. It really did pull at my enthusiasm for reading. My FAVOURITE book?! Wow, do I have to pick one? Impossible in all honesty as I have many that I love and don't favour over the other. To list three of them, I would have to say The Dark Hunter Series, By Sherrilyn Kenyon. The Seeker of Truth series by Terry Goodkind. And Any Nicholas Sparks book. (Except Dear John, hated that one.) I also love none fiction books, such as history books about Rome, Vikings, Samurai, War etc. I have no singular book that stands as number one. Even Harry Potter is right up there as some of my favourites. The book I am currently reading right now is called 'The Sea Road' by Margaret Elphinstone but I have to admit that I am struggling to get through it. It's not to my tastes and I find it a hard read, I won't be reading it again that's for sure and after this, I have another book waiting for me which I am very excited for. It is called 'Abandoned Breaths' by Alfa

Q: What is your favourite movie? And who is your favourite actor and actress? What is your favourite TV series? And your favourite singer and song? - Kevin

I struggle with questions like this because I really don't have a particular favourite, for me it is more like -groups- of favourites. What I will do is list three of each out of those I favour. So movies first: The Notebook, What Dreams May Come, Rocky 4. Three of my favourite actors: Norman Wisdom. Keanu Reeves, Jack Black. Three Favourite Actresses: Emilia Clarke (By far! So beautiful.) Melissa McCarthy, Katheryn Winnick. TV Series: Another hard one (There are so many!) Supernatural, Vikings, The Punisher, Walking Dead. Okay that's four, but I couldn't narrow it down to three. Singer and song is impossible to narrow down, there are too many, so what I will say is right now, I have 'Bed of Roses' by Bon Jovi playing and I am loving it.

Q: Why do you feel as if you are "ruined"? What have been your top 5 life lessons? All things being equal, is there any enticement that SHE could do that you would be willing to return to her side? - Gypsy

The basic definition of Ruined is: reduce (a building or place) to a state of decay, collapse, or disintegration. And I am that place. The mental mind games and heartbreak that I went through and continued to submit to because I loved somebody, reduced me into a state of decay. My soul collapsed and many things inside of me began to disintegrate. My confidence, My dreams, my hopes. All of it. What I went through caused great and irreparable damage to my heart and my ability to love. That is the why and the how of this ruined man.

I think that we all have our own lessons in life, what is a valuable lesson to one of us, may be useless to another. But for me, five lessons of life I have learned is: 1) Never believe in somebody else more than you believe in yourself because they will always let you down in the end, it is just a matter of time.. 2) The people you love, will hurt You 3) You cannot make a person love you back just by loving them enough for the both of you. 4) Cherry pie is so nice if you warm it up first, and then add a spoonful of cream to the top. 5) Souls Exist. They really do, but not everybody has one. And no, she could never come back now, it would never be the same and too many ghosts would get in the way of any realistic chance at a happy future. She made her bed, now she has to lie in it with all those other men, but never with me.

Q: How did you get started writing? - Kaitlyn

I've always enjoyed writing, It's a good way to release the crazy things that live and grow inside your head. I wrote stories since I was a child because I enjoyed writing about adventures that I would never get to experience (Mainly because those stories were about magical lands and fairy tales.) but I never wrote poetry. Shocking right? Poetry was never something I really even appreciated until I could relate to it. Once I finally began to understand poetry and see that it was far more than the picture that the words painted, I began to write my own. Poetry is full of innuendos, hidden messages, hidden feelings and emotions and I like that.

Q: Do you really write the way you feel, or do you feel the way you write? - Kane

I write the way I feel, and I feel the way I write. I write the words I feel inside, and I feel the words I bleed onto paper. Writing is feeling and there is no simpler answer than that.

Q: If you could go back in time and revisit a single moment, which moment would it be? - Meg

I have stared at this question for a long time now and I feel like I cannot in all honesty, accurately answer it. Because there are too many moments out there that hold the same value. One might think that I would go back to a time when the one I write about could be persuaded to stay. But I wouldn't, if they don't love you enough on their own accord, if they let you down and abandon you, then why would you waste such an opportunity on them? I certainly wouldn't, because she's not worth it any more. If I -had- to go back to a moment including her, it would be the day I met her, so I could turn around and walk away before our eyes ever connected. Moving on... I would love to go back to a moment where my dog was still alive, or all of the family dogs that we had. I would love to be able to sit with them all one more time. Feel their soft fur against my fingers, smell their scents. Cuddle and squeeze them so hard. That would be beautiful.

Q: Do you ever feel like you are the odd one out? How do you fit in? - Anonymous

Usually, when I walk into the room, I am most definitely the odd one out, But I am fine with that. I don't fit in, I never try to fit in and I do not want to fit in. None of us were born to fit in to anything, we are made from stars, and don't you see them at night? They aren't fitting into the darkness, they are shining brightly. They stand out. They are different. And so am I.

Q: How long did it take for you to find your own voice, your own path to existence, when your life was never planned on being lived alone? How do we move on and make something of all the brokenness? - Michael

I have always had my voice, that is one thing they could never take from me, but I know what it is to be lost. And I still am not entirely certainly that I am anything other than completely lost. We spend so much of ourselves building a life for two that when they leave us, we do not know how to convert that to one. But do it anyway, anything you planned to do with them, do it with You. Planned to go on that vacation with them? Go it alone. Wanted to watch that movie together? Watch it with you. Rediscover yourself and remember that you aren't broken because they hurt you, they are broken because they hurt You. Move on by understanding that you did everything right, you loved with all your heart and they were just not brave enough to do the same. You did not lose them, they lost You. You can keep on shining like a star, they will now have to make do with being blinded by your light. Move on because you are so much better than cowards and they don't deserve you, or your downfall. Rise.

PART THIRTEEN

EXCLUSIVES

"Take off that mask if you wish to speak to me, My life has no place for the fake words of a porcelain mask that hides the reality of you behind a field of painted roses."

Author's Note: As I was putting this book together, there were moments when I needed to stop, and write some poetry. Reading through all this work of mine reopened some old wounds and old scars. It brought back memories, of emotions and feelings that I never thought would be able to make me bleed again. But they did, and I needed to vent. So here are a couple of exclusives, pieces I wrote during the making of this book and have never been seen until now.

No Place At The Table

By Christopher Whitney

If you want to have the deepest and rawest of intimate conversations,

You have to leave your ego and your pride at the door.

Neither has a place at the table of real talk.

Cowardice Disguised as Survival

By Christopher Whitney

You really think that you know survival?

Darling, I -am- Survival.

What you call surviving, I call running. You cannot behave like a coward and constantly take the easy way out and then call it survival just because you don't want to accept that you have no courage.

Spend a day with me and you will see that survival is much more than running scared whilst claiming a victory. It is more than closing your eyes to what you don't want to see, and your ears to what you don't want to hear.

Survival is living, when everything else challenges you to give up and quit.

What you are doing is most certainly -not- survival, it is nothing more than dying before you are dead.

It is cowardice disguised as survival.

And that is a damn shame.

If you want to be a coward, go ahead and keep on running. That is fine. But you don't give up on somebody you love, even when you really want to.

You don't break a good person's heart for your own selfish gain and then call it surviving, because that is an insult to actual survivors all over this world.

If you were a survivor, you would have made it through the storm without quitting, but the moment you quit, you sacrificed your chance at being a survivor.

And you gave up, in the most heartless way.

I am a Survivor.

Because I survived your bullshit.

Wallpaper

By Christopher Whitney

They say that if somebody wants to leave, you should open the door for them...

But I Say...

Don't stop there.

Once they leave, close that door.

Lock it.

And brick up the doorway.

Then Wallpaper over it,

And hang a framed picture up on the wall where that door used to be.

I am mastering the art of battle,

within the warzone of my own soul.

I dominate insanity,

within the hospital corridors of my mind.

I stare down the pain,

and I laugh at the wounds.

They try to knock me down,

But I just keep getting back to my feet.

Christopher Whitney

PART FOURTEEN
FINAL WORDS

You have no idea

What it is like

to be so

utterly in love

with a complete stranger

We have reached this moment, the end of my first book. I want to take this moment to share some honesty and openness with you about my work on this book, and my work going forward.

Initially, This book was intended to be bigger, a lot bigger, but as I started to work on it I discovered that it would be too big. Thicker than the thickest book I have read in order to fit in -everything- that I have written and I decided that it was best to split them, into chapters and book one as you know, is called Chapter One. It was also my first time ever making a book and let me tell you, it's harder than I anticipated. The writing of it, was fine, but the formatting, coding, and all those messy technical parts were a struggle for me and if I had made this book bigger, I would likely have been overwhelmed by it all so I am very happy with the size of this book and how it turned out, I hope that all of you have enjoyed it and found a few favourite pieces inside.

My goal from here is to immediately begin working on Chapter Two, and then Chapter Three. There are more chapters than that in this book series, but after Chapter Three I might take a break from the poetry books to work on a novel that some of you may have heard of by now. It is called The Price of Souls. I also have another 'untitled' supernatural thriller that has been rolling around in my head. But I don't want to bore you with any of that right now.

I hope that by reading this book, it has helped you to understand some of those confusing and often tormenting feelings that can settle inside of us after a heartbreak. I hope that you were able to follow these first steps of a long journey with me, I hope that my words have offered some comfort or insight. At the very least, I hope that you have enjoyed my work and that you decide join us over on my Facebook page. I am aware that there appears to be other social outlets where my work has been appearing, and that is fine, but I just want to be clear that my Facebook page is the only official site of mine and I have no affiliation whatsoever with any other place that you may find my work.

I want to thank you all, for being here, for believing in me enough to invest into my work and read my book. Without my followers, without all of You, this book wouldn't even exist and I would probably be off somewhere, drowning at the bottom of a whiskey bottle. I hope you stay, and I look forward to continuing the rest of this journey together, So until next time, I wish you well.

Sincerely,

Christopher

Printed in Great Britain
by Amazon